THE
CHURCH MICE
AT CHRISTMAS

A TEMPLAR BOOK

This edition published in the UK in 2010 by Templar Publishing,
an imprint of The Templar Company Limited,
The Granary, North Street, Dorking, Surrey, RH4 1DN, UK
www.templarco.co.uk

First published in the UK in 1980 by Macmillan

Copyright © 1980 by Graham Oakley

3 5 7 9 10 8 6 4 2

ISBN 978-1-84877-065-2

Printed in China

THE
CHURCH MICE
AT CHRISTMAS

GRAHAM OAKLEY

templar publishing

MODERN CLASSICS

ONE MORNING a few days before Christmas,

Arthur and Humphrey, the leaders of the church mice,
were in the porch admiring the Christmas tree.
"It would be jolly nice to have a party," said Arthur suddenly.
"A real Christmas party with paper hats and crackers and games and things."
"Oh yes!" cried Humphrey. "And mince pies and trifle and custard
and blancmange and cream and jelly."

So it was all settled.

The first thing they had to do was to think of a way
of earning some money because parties can be
expensive. That puzzled them, until Arthur
happened to glance at the notice board. "That's it!"
he cried. "We'll raffle something."
They were just trying to think what the 'something'
could be when Sampson, the church cat, appeared.
The mice looked at him, and then they looked
at each other and smiled.

They made quite sure that they stood well out of
Sampson's reach when they told him they had
decided to raffle him. But in the end they managed
to convince him they were doing him a favour
really because whoever won him would *certainly*
be a cat-lover and treat him with *great* respect and
take him to a *lovely* home and give him an
enormous dinner, and anyway he could come back
to the vestry as soon as he liked. So they went
ahead with the raffle at once...

and soon the day of the draw arrived.

It went very well and everything happened exactly as
Arthur and Humphrey had predicted.

Well, perhaps not exactly,
but Sampson was fairly philosophical about it.
"After all," he said to himself as he slunk back to the
vestry an hour or so later, "any cat that's stupid
enough to take a vow never to harm mice
deserves what he gets."

When Sampson found them,
the mice were still discussing how best
to spend the raffle money.

Later that evening, however, the raffle winners discovered that their prize had run away.
But they weren't too worried because they knew where they would find him, roughly.

And Humphrey showed them precisely. He said he was sorry that the prize hadn't given satisfaction
and although he couldn't, under any circumstances, refund their ticket money, he was able to offer them
the vestry dustpan instead, which was much better value than a mere cat, even if the handle was missing.

But the couple preferred Sampson.
They tried to wheedle him out with winning
smiles and honeyed words, but Sampson
wouldn't be wheedled.

So eventually, despite what Humphrey had said
about not giving refunds, they took their money
and went home. The mice were really depressed
about this because without the money there would
be no party. Humphrey muttered that though it
wasn't in his nature to criticise, there was a certain
whiskery, ginger individual who would do well to
look up the word *selfish* in the dictionary. But he
didn't say it loud enough for Sampson to hear.

To cheer themselves up, Arthur and Humphrey
decided to go across to the vicarage to watch
television. On the way they racked their brains to
think of another way to make some money, but
without success. Later on, however, they saw
something that sparked off an idea.

And the next day, they rounded up the mice with
the loudest voices. They spent the whole morning
practising their scales and the whole afternoon
sorting out the pronunciation of 'Wenceslas', and
by the time it was dark, they were ready.

Carol singing had seemed a really good plan in the vestry...

But as Humphrey said afterwards, "Everybody knows that the best laid schemes of mice and thingummies often end in a mess."

Those who didn't were learning – fast. Arthur and Humphrey fled through a shop door...

and inside they tried a rather clever trick. It would have worked, too,
if a customer hadn't thought they would make such lovely little stocking-fillers.

From then on it was just one thing after another. Fortunately, Arthur kept his head...

and managed to get them aboard a passing train. Humphrey complained that they should have enquired where it was going first, but Arthur said they would find out soon enough. They never did.

But just when it looked as if they had come to the end,
Arthur spotted the very thing for a quick getaway...

although it turned out to be a pretty close-run thing.

Once outside, the mice all met up again and managed to slip away unnoticed into the crowd.

The journey back to the vestry was dreadful.
Everyone was gloomy because of the failure of the expedition, and it didn't help matters
to have to listen to Humphrey explaining his new theory about how Christmas Day
should change places with August Bank Holiday so that people wouldn't have to tramp
through the snow to do their Christmas shopping.

It took ages for them to get their wind back, but
when they had, Arthur announced that since they
hadn't made a single penny out of their carol
singing, there wouldn't be a party after
all. At this, the mice looked so miserable
that Arthur, after a few moments'
thought, told them they should
cheer up because he still had a
very pleasant surprise in store
for them.

After that, he and Humphrey whispered together
for a long time. Then, as quietly as possible,
they filled a paper bag with odds and ends from
the choirboys' lockers, woke Sampson and tiptoed
out of the vestry while nobody was looking.
Outside, Arthur assured them that they would
find whatever else they needed in the
parson's garden shed.

On the way back to the vestry, a most wonderful thing happened to them. Even Humphrey was speechless for two seconds. Then he said, "Good evening, Father Christmas sir. I am Humphrey, and what I want for Christmas is a record player, a quartz watch, twenty bags of jelly babies, a pair of two-tone football boots, a—"

"And what I would like..." began Arthur.

"—radio," continued Humphrey, "a dozen walnut whips...

The Beano Annual, a yo-yo, three boxes of fudge,
an electric guitar, a—"
"And what I would…" began Arthur.
"—big television," Humphrey continued,
"six boxes of cheese spread, a cuckoo clock, a calculator
and a packet of custard creams."

"And what I…" began Arthur.
"Well, that will do for now," said Humphrey, "because
the sergeant is obviously in a hurry to give you his list.
So if Your Worship will just make a note of my address—"
and he shouted it out, very slowly so that there
could be no mistake.
"Right then," he finished, "we'll expect Your Highness at
nine o'clock tonight, sharp. Carry on, Sergeant."

They decided they might as well go on pretending to be Father Christmas even though the real one was now going to visit them, because it would amuse the mice and fill up the time until he arrived. Unfortunately, it wasn't the mice who seemed to find them amusing...

so their return to the vestry was anything but the very pleasant surprise that Arthur had promised...

though they made up for it by telling the mice about their meeting with Father Christmas
and explaining that he would be coming to the vestry at nine o'clock. Everyone started to get ready at once.

Meanwhile, a reward for the persons who had helped to capture the burglar had arrived at Wortlethorpe Police Station, and the sergeant, who had heard Humphrey shouting out his address, promised to deliver it himself.

Back in the vestry, it wasn't long before everything was spick and span,
and by the time the church clock struck nine, the mice were ready and waiting.

At the same moment in Wortlethorpe Police Station, the sergeant was struck with a brilliant idea. *If great detectives can wear disguises to catch villains,* he thought to himself, *why can't I?* So he borrowed the burglar's Father Christmas outfit, and when he looked in the mirror he scarcely recognised himself. "It's a stroke of genius," he muttered. "I'll be a chief inspector before you can say Sherlock Holmes!"

In the vestry the mice heard the clock strike quarter past nine, and Arthur and Humphrey started to get worried.
At the police station the sergeant was just setting off on his rounds, and as he had to pass the church,
he decided to deliver the mice's reward.

When the clock struck half past nine, Arthur and Humphrey began to fear for their safety.
Humphrey started to stammer that Father Christmas was probably having trouble with his reindeer
or something, but the mice were in no mood for excuses.

And by a quarter to ten, the mood in the vestry
was very ugly indeed. Sampson was about to step in
and do something about it when suddenly
the door creaked open and...

For a long time after Father Christmas had gone,
the mice just sat and stared, murmuring things like
"Gosh" and "Golly" and "Crumbs".

Then, with shrieks of excitement,
they all rushed to see what he had brought them.
What they saw was everything that anybody could
possibly want for a Christmas party.

And what a party they had. It was good enough to make Humphrey forget all about televisions and yo-yos and things. In fact it was so good that they were all ill for three days after it, and when it was over there was enough left for the choirboys to have a party of their own and be ill for three days as well.

Even after that, the mice were still able to find a box of crystallised fruits, a tin of asparagus and a jar of pickled walnuts, and since it was the season of goodwill to all men, they decided to give these to the parson.

But then Humphrey informed them that years and years of intensive scientific research had proved conclusively that parsons don't like crystallised fruits. So they kept those, and had a feast on New Year's Eve, just to round off the year nicely.

THE END

GRAHAM OAKLEY

AND THE CHURCH MICE SERIES

When Graham Oakley began THE CHURCH MOUSE,
he intended to create a series of stories about different public
buildings in Wortlethorpe, but the first book was so
successful, that he never got on to the library!

Instead, the stories of Sampson and the church mice became
modern children's classics, garnering critical acclaim and
capturing the imagination of a generation of children.

Between 1972 and 2000, Graham wrote and illustrated
fourteen CHURCH MICE tales. The series was nominated
for two Kate Greenaway Medals, won a *New York Times* Best
Illustrated Children's Book award and sold over one and
a half million books worldwide.